NORTHANGER
ABBEY

NORTHANGER ABBEY

Jane Austen

Om
KIDZ

An imprint of Om Books International

First published in 2019 by

Om
KIDZ Om Books International

Corporate & Editorial Office
A-12, Sector 64, Noida 201 301
Uttar Pradesh, India
Phone: +91 120 477 4100
Email: editorial@ombooks.com
Website: www.ombooksinternational.com

Sales Office
107, Ansari Road, Darya Ganj
New Delhi 110 002, India
Phone: +91 11 4000 9000
Email: sales@ombooks.com
Website: www.ombooks.com

© Om Books International 2019

Retold by Swayam Ganguly

ISBN: 978-93-85031-60-1

Printed in India

10 9 8 7 6 5 4 3 2 1

Contents

1. Making of a Heroine   7
2. The Ball   17
3. Enter Mr. Tilney   27
4. The Thorpes   41
5. Love for Novels   51
6. A Reunion   65
7. The Dance   85
8. Thorpe Plays Dirty   105
9. An Engagement   127
10. Captain Tilney   139
11. Isabella Behaves Strangely   155
12. Northanger Abbey   167
13. The Storm   179
14. The Mystery of Mrs. Tilney   187
15. A Sense of Shame   201
16. A Trip to Woodston   211
17. Sent Home   221
18. All's Well that Ends Well   233
About the Author   236
Characters   236
Questions   237

Chapter One

Making of a Heroine

No one who had seen Catherine Morland in her infancy would have ever imagined that she was born to be a heroine. Her father was a respected clergyman named Richard, neither poor nor neglected. He was not a handsome man. He had an independent spirit and was not prone to locking up his daughters indoors.

Her mother was a plain, useful woman who was blessed with a good temper and constitution. When after three sons she gave birth to Catherine, everybody expected her to die. But she lived on instead, to have six more children, raised them successfully and enjoyed excellent health herself.

A family of ten children will always be considered a fine family, but the Morlands were rather plain. Catherine was no exception. She had a thin, awkward figure, a yellowish colourless skin, dark lank hair and strong features. Her mind was also unfit for heroism. Catherine was fond of boys' sports like cricket, rather than playing with dolls. She was also least interested in the more heroic pleasures of infancy like feeding a canary-bird, nursing a dormouse or watering a rose-bush.

If Catherine collected flowers at all, it was largely for mischief and she always preferred to pluck the forbidden ones. She could not learn or comprehend anything before she was taught; and sometimes not even then because she was so inattentive and stupid at times. Her mother took three months to teach her just to repeat the 'Beggar's Petition', which her next sister, Sally, could say better than Catherine. But Catherine was not always stupid and learnt the fable of 'The Hare and Many Friends' as quickly as any other girl in England.

Her mother wanted her to learn music; Catherine was positive she would like it as she loved tinkling the

keys of the old, forlorn spinet. Hence, music lessons began when Catherine was eight years old. But after a year she hated it, and was allowed by her mother to discontinue. The day the music master was dismissed was the happiest day in Catherine's life. Her taste for drawing was not remarkable either; she drew houses and trees, hens and chickens in a strikingly similar manner.

Her father taught her accounts and writing, and her mother taught her French. Catherine's proficiency in these subjects was ordinary and she was prone to shirk her lessons at any opportunity that provided itself. But even though she had a strange, inexplicable character, a ten-year-old Catherine did not possess a bad heart or temper. She was rarely a stubborn child, seldom quarrelsome and extremely kind to the little ones. But she was wild and noisy and hated cleanliness, and being confined indoors. There was nothing Catherine liked better than rolling down the green slope at the back of the house.

Mrs. Morland was a good woman and wanted to see her children be everything they should be. But she was

so busy tending to the little ones that her elder daughters were left to fend for themselves. It was not wonderful that a fourteen-year-old Catherine preferred outdoor sports and running about the country to books because no useful knowledge could be derived from them, and they were all story and no reflection.

When she was fifteen, Catherine's appearance witnessed a stark change. She began to curl her hair, and desired for balls; her complexion improved, her features were softened by colour and weight, her eyes became more animated, and her figure noticeable. The love of dirt was replaced by an inclination for finery, and Catherine became clean as she turned smarter. Her parents remarked on this personal improvement that gave Catherine much pleasure. To be called 'almost pretty' is a huge compliment for a girl who has spent the first fifteen years of her life looking simply plain.

From age fifteen to seventeen, Catherine was training to be a heroine, reading such works that heroines must read to be armed with quotations that would prove useful in life. From Pope, she learnt to censure those who 'bear

about the mockery of woe'; from Gray, that 'many a flower is born to blush unseen, and waste its fragrance on the desert air'; from Thomson, that 'it is a delightful task to teach the young idea how to shoot'. She gained much information from Shakespeare. Although she could not write sonnets, she learned how to read them. She had no idea about drawing, and as she had no lover to portray, was unaware of her poverty. Catherine turned seventeen but there was no lord or baronet in the neighbourhood who would ensure that she became a heroine. But when a young lady is to be a heroine, nothing can prevent her. Something inevitably happens to throw a hero in her way.

Chapter Two

The Ball

Mr. Allen, the owner of the majority of the property of Fullerton, the village in Wiltshire where the Morlands resided, was ordered to Bath as a remedy for gout. His lady, a good humoured woman who was fond of Miss Morland, invited her to accompany them. Her parents gave their consent and Catherine was all happiness.

When the hour for departure to Bath drew near, the maternal anxiety of Mrs. Morland kept rising. She had alarming premonitions of evil and her heart was full of sadness at this separation. The last day or two when mother and daughter were together, Mrs. Morland cried her heart out. Then her wise lips cautioned her daughter against the violence of noblemen and baronets

where young women were concerned. The fact that Mrs. Morland knew very little about noblemen and baronets compounded her fears.

Everything about Catherine's journey to Bath was indulged in by the Morlands with moderation and calmness. Her father handed her only ten guineas, with a promise for more when she wanted it. The journey to Bath was an uneventful one, and Catherine was delighted when they arrived. Her eyes were everywhere as they drove to the hotel in Pulteney Street.

Mrs. Allen was such a woman that whoever encountered her was surprised that any man could have liked her enough to have married her. She lacked beauty, manner, genius and accomplishment. What probably justified the sensible, intelligent Mr. Allen's choice was her air of a gentlewoman, her quietude and good temper. In a way, she was perfect to introduce a young lady into public, being fond of public appearances herself. She was passionate about dress and fashion and she provided Catherine with a dress of the latest fashion. Catherine made some purchases herself, and the important evening arrived when she would be ushered into the Upper Rooms. The

best hand cut and dressed her hair. She was dressed carefully and both Mrs. Allen and her maid declared that she looked perfect.

Mrs. Allen took so long in dressing that it was late when they finally entered the ballroom. The room being crowded, the two ladies squeezed in as best as they could. The crowd seemed to increase as they went further and all they could see were the high feathers of the dancers amidst the huge crowd. Luckily, they managed to reach the passage behind the highest bench, where the crowd was comparatively less than below. It was a splendid sight and Catherine longed to dance but sadly, she knew no one. 'I wish you could dance, my dear,' Mrs. Allen stated every now and then to comfort Catherine. 'I wish you could get a partner.'

It was disappointing that they had to squeeze out with the rest for tea soon. There was no sign of Mr. Allen, and they had only each other to talk to.

'How uncomfortable it is, not to know anyone here.' Catherine whispered after they were seated. 'Yes, my dear,' Mrs. Allen replied in a serene manner. 'It is very uncomfortable indeed; it seems that the gentlemen and ladies at this table think that we are forcing ourselves into their party.'

'That is very disagreeable, indeed. I wish we knew some people here.'

'Well, I wish the same. We could talk to someone, then.'

'True, my dear. The Skinners were here last year. I wish they were here now.'

'Should we leave? There are no tea things for us here.'
'I think we should sit still, as one gets tumbled in such a crowd.'

One of their neighbours finally offered them some tea and it was gladly accepted, leading to a small conversation with the gentleman who offered it. This was the only time when someone spoke to them in the course of the evening, before Mr. Allen joined them when the dance was over.

'Miss Moreland, I hope you have had an agreeable ball,' he stated.

'Very agreeable, indeed,' Catherine replied, trying to stifle a yawn.

'She could have danced had we been able to find her a partner. I wish the Skinners or the Parrys were here so she could have danced with George Parry.'

'I hope we shall do better another evening,' Mr. Allen said comfortingly.

The company started dispersing after the dance, and it was time for the heroine, who had not played a major part in the events of the evening, to be noticed and admired. No one stared at her with rapturous wonder, no eager whispers happened, and neither was she termed a divinity. But she was looked at and admired, and two gentlemen called her a pretty girl. Catherine found the evening pleasanter immediately, and her humble vanity was satisfied.

Chapter Three

Enter Mr. Tilney

Regular duties presented themselves each morning; shops needed to be visited, some new part of the town needed to be looked at, the Pump Room had to be attended. They paraded up and down here, speaking to no one. Mrs. Allen wished to make lots of acquaintances at Bath, but failed.

But when they appeared at the Lower Rooms, fortune was more favourable to our heroine. She was introduced by the master of ceremonies as partner to a young gentleman called Tilney. He appeared twenty-five, was tall, had intelligent and lively eyes, and was pleasing to the eye. Catherine felt herself to be lucky, and although conversation was not possible as they danced, she discovered that he was as agreeable as she had thought him to be when they were seated together at tea.

He spoke fluently and spiritedly, and the pleasantness in his manner interested Catherine.

'Have you been long in Bath, madam?' He enquired in a simpering manner.

'About a week, sir,' Catherine replied, trying not to laugh.

'Really?' He asked in astonishment.

'Why are you surprised, sir?'

'Why indeed?' He stated in his natural voice. 'Have you never been here before?'

'Never, sir.'

'Have you honoured the Upper Rooms yet?'

'Yes, sir. I was there last Monday.'

'Have you visited the theatre?'

'Yes, sir. I was at the play on Tuesday.'

'The concert?'

'Yes, sir. On Wednesday.'

'Do you like Bath?'

'Yes.'

'I must give a smirk now, and then we shall be rational again.'

Catherine turned her head away, not knowing if she should laugh.

'I think I shall make a poor figure in your journal tomorrow,' he declared.

'My journal!'

'Yes, I know just what you will say: Friday, went to the Lower Rooms; wore my sprigged muslin robe with blue trimmings and plain black shoes, but was strangely harassed by a weird, half-witted man, who wanted to make me dance with him, distressing me with his nonsense.'

'I shall say no such thing, indeed.'

'May I tell you what you should say?'

'If you please.'

'I danced with a very agreeable young man introduced by Mr. King, conversed a lot with him. He seems an extraordinary genius, and I hope I may know more of him. That is what I wish you'd say, madam.'

'Maybe I keep no journal.'

'Maybe we are not sitting together in this room. It is equally possible to doubt such things, too. Not keep a journal? How will your absent cousins know about your

activities in Bath without one? How will the civilities and compliments be remembered? How will you remember your numerous dresses, the diverse ways of the curl of your hair, and the particular state of your complexion? My dear madam, I am not ignorant of the ways of young ladies as you think me to be. The delightful habit of journalising daily events enables the easy style of writing that ladies are often celebrated for. That is why the talent of writing agreeable letters is acknowledged to be best by the female hand. Nature might have been helpful, but I'm positive that the practice of keeping a journal played a major role.'

'I have often doubted if ladies wrote better than gentlemen.'

'I think letter-writing is faultless among women except in three particulars.'

'What are they?'

'A general lack of subject, a total inattention to stops, and a rather frequent ignorance of grammar.'

'Upon my word! No wonder I was skeptical about the compliment. You do not think much highly of us.'

'I do not think that it is a general rule that women write better letters than men, or that they sing better duets, or draw better landscapes. Where matters of taste are concerned, excellence is more or less divided between the sexes.'

Mrs. Allen interrupted them. 'My dear Catherine,' she said. 'Please take this pin out of my sleeve. It has torn a hole already, I'm afraid. It is a favourite gown, although costing only nine shillings a yard.'

'I would have guessed that exactly, madam,' Mr. Tilney offered, gazing at the muslin.

'Do you understand muslins, sir?'

'Particularly well. I always purchase my own cravats and my sister has always trusted me in choosing a gown for her. I bought one for her the other day, and every lady who saw it, declared it to be a great bargain. I paid five shillings a yard for it, and true Indian muslin it was, too.'

Mrs. Allen was awestruck by his genius. 'Men take so little notice of these things,' she declared. 'I can never get Mr. Allen to differentiate between my gowns. You must be a great comfort to your sister, sir.'

'I hope so, madam.'

'What do you think of Miss Morland's gown?'

'It is very pretty, madam,' he said, examining it seriously. 'But I don't think it will wash well. I'm afraid it will fray.'

Catherine laughed, but Mrs. Allen agreed with him. 'I told Miss Morland so when she bought it.'

'But then you are aware, madam, that muslin is never wasted. It can always be made into a cap, cloak or a handkerchief.'

'Bath is indeed a charming place, sir, with so many good shops. Sadly, we are way off in the country, and Salisbury is eight miles away. Here, one can step outside and get whatever you want in five minutes.'

Mr. Tilney listened to Mrs. Allen politely on the subject of muslins till the dancing resumed. Catherine thought he indulged himself too much in the affairs of others.

'What are you thinking so seriously?' He asked, as they walked back to the ballroom. 'Not of your partner, I hope?'

'I was not thinking of anything,' Catherine replied,

colouring instantly.

'That is clever, but I'd rather be told that you won't tell me.'

'Well then, I will not.'

'Thank you, as I am authorised to tease you on this subject whenever we meet, and nothing improves intimacy as much.'

They danced again, and when the evening ended, Catherine couldn't help thinking about him. It is not certain if she dreamt of him, as like a celebrated writer stated, no young lady is justified of falling in love before a gentleman has professed his love for her. It must be improper for a young lady to dream about a gentleman before he has dreamt about her.

Mr. Allen had made enquiries about Mr. Tilney and was rather satisfied to learn that he was a clergyman, hailing from a very respectable family in Gloucestershire.

Chapter Four

The Thorpes

Catherine rushed to the Pump Room the next day with unusual eagerness, hoping to meet Mr. Tilney there. But he was absent.

'What a delightful place Bath is,' Mrs. Allen stated, as they seated themselves near the great clock. 'How pleasant it would be if we had any acquaintance here.'

This sentiment had been uttered so many times in vain that Mrs. Allen could not have possibly hoped for it to hold more promise. But her untiring diligence was rewarded when a lady of about her own age addressed her after ten minutes of attentive scrutiny.

'I think I am not mistaken, madam; it is a long time since I've had the pleasure of seeing you after all, but is not your name Allen?'

After Mrs. Allen replied in the affirmative, the stranger stated her name as Thorpe. Mrs. Allen instantly recognised her former schoolmate, whom she had seen just once after their respective marriages, many years ago. The joy on this meeting was great, as they had known nothing of each other for fifteen long years. They spoke at length, and Mrs. Thorpe did most of the talking, as she extolled on the virtues of her many children.

'There are my dear girls,' Mrs. Thorpe exclaimed as three smart-looking ladies arrived arm in arm. 'The tallest is Isabella, also the eldest and the handsomest.'

The Miss Thorpes were introduced, and so was Miss Morland.

'Miss Morland is so much like her brother,' Isabella exclaimed, and her mother agreed whole-heartedly.

Catherine was surprised momentarily, before she recalled that her eldest brother James Morland had formed a friendship with Thorpe, a young man from his college. He had spent the last week of the Christmas vacation with the Thorpes. The Miss Thorpes were now desirous of being better acquainted with Catherine, although they already considered her a friend thanks to

the friendship of their brothers. Catherine was delighted as Isabella led her away by the arm. She almost forgot about Mr. Tilney as she spoke to Isabella. They say friendship is the best balm for disappointed love!

The conversation between the two young women featured dress, balls and flirtations among other things. Miss Thorpe, four years older than Miss Morland, had a distinct advantage as she was capable of comparing the balls at Bath with those at Tunbridge. She was also aware of the fashions of London, and could advise her new friend over matters of attire. Catherine admired these powers, and felt an ever growing affection towards Miss Thorpe.

When they left the Pump Room, Miss Thorpe decided to escort Miss Morland to Mr. Allen's house. There, they parted happily after learning that they would meet again at the theatre that night, and say their prayers in the same chapel the next morning. Catherine was grateful in gaining such a friend. Mrs. Thorpe was a widow, albeit not a very rich one. But she was a good woman and an indulgent mother. Her eldest daughter had been

blessed with great personal beauty, and her younger ones did rather well by dressing like and imitating their eldest sister.

At the theatre, Catherine did acknowledge the nods and smiles of Miss Thorpe, but much of her attention was engaged in looking to spot Mr. Tilney in every box. But she looked in vain! Catherine hoped to be more fortunate the next day. It was a beautiful morning. A fine Sunday empties the houses of Bath of all its residents, who walk about remarking to each other how beautiful the day is.

After the conclusion of the divine services, the Thorpes and Allens joined each other eagerly. They left for the Crescent from the Pump Room. Catherine and Isabella enjoyed each other's company, but the former was disappointed not to catch a glimpse of the man she wanted to see so dearly. He must have left Bath! But he hadn't mentioned that his stay would be so short. This sort of mystery, so becoming of a hero, aroused Catherine's interest, and she was anxious to know more of him. She could learn nothing from the Thorpes, as they had been in Bath for just two days before they had met her.

Catherine confided in Isabella, who assured her that he must be a charming young man, and must surely be delighted with her dear Catherine. Hence, he would return soon. Isabella liked him more for being a clergyman, and she confessed that she was very partial to the profession. Mrs. Allen was now overjoyed, and quite happy with Bath. She had finally found an acquaintance, and that too lucky enough to meet the family of an old friend.

Meanwhile, Catherine and Isabella's friendship grew in leaps and bounds. They called each other by their Christian names now, and always walked arm in arm. They were inseparable, and if a rainy morning denied them the chance to meet, they would brave the rain and dirt to meet, shut themselves up indoors, and read novels together.

Chapter Five

Love for Novels

The two friends met in the Pump Room one morning, eight or nine days after being acquainted with each other. 'My dearest creature, what could have possibly made you so late?' Isabella exclaimed after Catherine arrived. 'I have been waiting for you for an eternity.'

'Have you, indeed!' Catherine replied. 'I am very sorry for being late, although I thought I was on time. It is just one. I hope you haven't been waiting long?'

'Oh, ten ages at least. But I'm sure I've been waiting for half-an-hour. But let us go to the other end of the room as I have so much to say to you. Firstly, I was scared it would rain this morning just as I had left. That would have caused me a lot of pain! Do you know that I spotted

the prettiest hat in a shop window in Milsom Street right now? It was very similar to yours, except that it had coquelicot ribbons instead of green. I simply longed for it. But tell me Catherine, what have you been up to since morning? Have you gone on with *Udolpho*?'

'Yes, I have been reading it ever since I woke up. I have got to the black veil.'

'Indeed? How delightful! Oh, I would not tell you what is behind the black veil for the world! Aren't you eager to know?'

'Of course. What can it be? But do not tell me as I do not want to be told on any account. I'm sure it is a skeleton, Laurentina's skeleton! I am simply delighted with this book! I would like to spend my entire life reading it. If I didn't have to meet you, I would not have abandoned the book for all the world.'

'Oh, dear creature! I am so obliged to you. We shall read *The Italian* together after you have finished reading *Udolpho*. I have made a list of ten or twelve of the same kind for you.'

'Have you? Oh, how glad I am! What are they?'

'Let me take out my pocketbook. Here they are, *Castle of Wolfenbach, Clermont, Mysterious Warnings, Necromancer of the Black Forest, Orphan of the Rhine* and *Horrid Mysteries.*'

'Yes. But are you sure that they are all horrid?'

'Perfectly sure. A friend of mine named Miss Andrews, one of the sweetest creatures in the world, has read all of them. I wish you knew her, as she is delightful. I think she is as beautiful as an angel, and I am so irritated with men for not admiring her! I scold them all about it!'

'Do you scold them for not admiring her?'

'Yes. There is nothing that I wouldn't do for my real friends. It is not my nature to love people by halves, and my attachments are always excessively strong. I refused to dance with Captain Hunt once if he did not consider Miss Andrews to be as beautiful as an angel. The men think that we are not capable of real friendship, and I am determined to display to them the difference. If someone would speak slightingly of you, I would fire up in a moment. But that is very unlikely, my dear, as you are bound to be a great favourite with the men.'

'Oh dear!' Catherine exclaimed, colouring instantly. 'How can you say so?'

'Well, I know you so well now. You have so much animation, which is exactly what is lacking in Miss Andrews. I must confess that there is something about her that is amazingly insipid. Oh, I forgot to tell you something! Just after we parted yesterday, I spotted a young man looking at you rather earnestly. I am sure that he is in love with you!'

Catherine coloured again, speaking in denial, and Isabella laughed. 'It is the truth, upon my honour. But I see that you are indifferent to everyone's attention, with the exception of a certain gentleman, who shall be nameless. Well, I cannot blame you.'

She spoke more seriously now, 'I can understand your feelings. If the heart is truly attached, one is little pleased with someone else's attention.'

'But you should not persuade me that I think a lot about Mr. Tilney, as I may never see him again.'

'My dear, do not talk like that. I am sure that thought would make you very miserable, indeed.'

'No, I should not. I would be lying if I said I wasn't pleased with him, but while I have *Udolpho* to read, I feel nothing can make me miserable. Oh, that dreadful black veil! Oh, Isabella! I am sure Laurentina's skeleton lurks behind it.'

'I find it odd that you haven't read *Udolpho* before. I suppose Mrs. Morland objects to novels.'

'No, she doesn't. In fact, she often reads *Sir Charles Grandison* herself. But I'm afraid new books do not fall in our way.'

'*Sir Charles Grandison*? That's an amazingly horrid book, isn't it? I recall Miss Andrews being unable to get through the first volume.'

'Well, it's very unlike *Udolpho*. But I do think it's an entertaining book.'

'Do you indeed? That's surprising, as I thought it to be unreadable. But, dearest Catherine, have you decided what to wear on your head tonight? I am quite determined to be dressed exactly like you. The men do take notice of that sometimes, you know.'

'But it does not mean that they do,' Catherine stated sweetly.

'I make it a rule never to mind whatever they say as they can be very impertinent if not treated spiritedly, and I make them keep their distance.'

'I have never observed that as they behave well enough with me.'

'Oh! But they give themselves such airs. They are the most conceited creatures in this world, and consider themselves to be so important. I have always meant to ask you but never have, what is your favourite complexion in a man? Dark or fair?'

'Between both, I think. Neither fair nor dark. Brown!'

'That is exactly Mr. Tilney. I haven't forgotten your description of him- 'brown skin, with dark eyes and hair.' Well, my taste differs, as I like light eyes, and a sallow complexion. Do not betray me if you meet one of your acquaintances answering that description.'

'Betray you? What do you mean?'

'I have said too much. Let's drop the subject.'

Catherine was amazed, but agreed, and after a moment's silence, Isabella urged her friend to move away from the end of the room as she declared that two men were staring at her for half an hour. They walked

away from there and Isabella enquired if the men were following them. Catherine informed her that the men had left the Pump Room.

'Which way have they gone?' Isabella enquired, turning around hastily. 'One was a rather good looking young man.'

'Towards the churchyard.'

'I am so glad I have got rid of them! Now, do you want to accompany me to Edgar's Buildings to see my new hat?'

Catherine agreed, adding, 'But we might overtake the two young men. If we leave after a few moments, there will be no danger of seeing them at all.'

'I assure you that I shan't be paying them any compliments. I have no intention of treating men with such respect as that only spoils them.'

Catherine could not oppose such reasoning, and to demonstrate Miss Thorpe's independent spirit, and her resolution of humbling the opposite sex, they set off immediately. They walked as fast as they could, pursuing the two young men.

Chapter Six

A Reunion

In half a minute, they had reached the archway through the Pump House, opposite Union Passage, where they were stopped. Anyone familiar with Bath might recall the difficulties of crossing Cheap Street at this point. It is an impertinent street, unfortunately connected with the great London and Oxford roads. Not a day passes when parties of young ladies and men are not detained on one side, because of the numerous carts, carriages and horsemen.

Their progress was arrested by the approach of a gig on a bad pavement. The coachman drove with great rage and carelessness, endangering his own life, and that of his horse and companion. 'How I detest these horrible

gigs!' Isabella exclaimed. This detestation, however, was short lived. 'Oh how delightful!' Isabella exclaimed after just a moment. 'Mr. Morland and my brother!'

'James! Good heavens!' Catherine exclaimed.

The horse was checked with great violence, almost throwing him on his haunches, and the gentlemen jumped out. Catherine received her brother with the greatest pleasure, even though this meeting was totally unexpected. He did the same, as he was equally attached to her. The bright eyes of Miss Thorpe were constantly seeking his attention, and he complied, with a mixture of joy and embarrassment. If Catherine would have been more experienced in judging other people's feelings, instead of being engrossed in her own, she might have noticed that her brother thought her friend was very pretty.

John Thorpe, who had been giving orders about the horses, joined them after that. He was a stout, young man of medium height, with a plain face, and an ungraceful form.

'How long do you think we have been travelling from Tetbury, Miss Morland?' He enquired. Catherine admitted that she was unaware of the distance.

'It's twenty-three miles,' her brother declared.

'Three and twenty?' Thorpe exclaimed. 'Why, it is not an inch less than twenty-five miles.'

Morland argued with the help of knowledge gained from road-books, innkeepers and milestones, but Thorpe was dismissive of it all, claiming that his sense of distance was accurate. 'I know it's five and twenty by the time we have been doing it. It is half-past one now and we drove out of Tetbury at eleven. No man in England can make my horse travel in less than ten miles an hour in harness. That makes it exactly twenty-five miles.'

'It was ten o'clock when we set out from Tetbury,' Morland protested.

'It was eleven, upon my soul,' Thorpe insisted. 'I counted every stroke. Miss Morland, this brother of yours will persuade me out of my senses. But look at my horse! Did you ever see such a speedier animal? Such true blood! Look at that creature!'

Catherine watched the servant mount the carriage and drive off.

'Well, he does look rather hot!' She remarked.

'Hot! He did not turn a hair till we neared Walcot Church! Look at his forehand; look at those loins; see how he moves; that horse simply cannot go less than ten miles an hour. You can tie his legs but he will still move on. What do you think of my gig, Miss Morland? It is a neat one, isn't it? It's a month new, town-built, and well hung. It was built for a Christchurch man who was a friend of mine. A very good fellow, really. He ran it for a few weeks and I happened to meet him one day, driving into Oxford. He asked me if I wanted it for fifty guineas and it was such a good bargain that I couldn't refuse.'

'I'm sure it was,' Catherine replied. 'I know so little of such things that I cannot judge.'

'I dare say I might have got it cheaper. But I hate haggling, and poor Freeman needed and wanted cash.'

'That was so good-natured of you!'

'Yes, when one does a kind thing to a friend, one can't haggle.'

It was decided that the gentlemen would accompany the ladies to Edgar's Buildings, to pay their respects to Mrs. Thorpe. John Thorpe stayed close to Catherine,

and soon resumed the conversation about his gig. 'Miss Morland, some people might consider it cheap, as I might have sold it for ten guineas more the very next day. Jackson of Oriel bid me sixty instantly. Morland was with me then.'

'Yes, but you forget that your horse was included in the offer,' Morland said, overhearing his friend.

'Oh! I wouldn't sell my horse for a hundred! Are you fond of an open carriage, Miss Morland?'

'Yes. I must admit that I have hardly had an opportunity of being in one, but I'm especially fond of it.'

'I shall be glad to drive you out in mine every day.'

'Thank you,' Catherine said in some distress, doubting the courtesy of accepting such an offer.

'I shall drive you up Lansdown Hill tomorrow.'

'Thank you, but won't your horse need rest?'

'Rest! He has only come twenty-three miles today. Nonsense! Nothing ruins a horse more than rest. I shall exercise mine for at least four hours every day while I'm here.'

'Indeed! That will make it forty miles a day.'

'Forty or fifty, how do I care? I shall drive you up Lansdown tomorrow.'

'How delightful!' Isabella exclaimed, turning around. 'I envy you, dear Catherine. I'm afraid, brother, you will not have room for a third person.'

'A third? No, no; I did not arrive at Bath to drive my sisters about; that would be a good joke though! Morland will have to take care of you.'

This caused a conversation between the other two, but Catherine did not hear it as Isabelle's discourse focused on praise or criticism of the face of every woman they encountered. It was a subject that did not arouse Catherine's interest.

'Have you read *Udalpho*, Mr. Thorpe?' She asked.

'*Udalpho*? Good Lord! No; I never read novels; I have something else to do. Novels are so full of nonsense, and there hasn't been a tolerably decent one that's come out since *Tom Jones*, except *The Monk* perhaps. I read that the other day. But regarding the rest of them, they are the stupidest things to be created.'

'I think you will like *Udalpho*, if you read it. It is a very interesting novel.'

'Not I! If I read any, it shall be by Mrs. Radcliffe. Her novels are amusing enough, and worth reading. There is some fun and nature in them.'

'*Udolpho* was written by Mrs. Radcliffe,' Catherine stated hesitantly, for fear that he be mortified.

'Was it? I am not sure. Yes, I remember. I was thinking of that other stupid book, written by that woman they make so much of a fuss about; the one who married the French emigrant.'

'You mean *Camilla* I suppose?'

'Yes, that is the one; such unnatural stuff! An old man playing at see-saw. I soon discovered after looking over the first volume that it would not do. I had guessed the sort of stuff it must be before I had even seen it, as I had heard about her marrying an emigrant. I was sure I would be unable to finish it.'

'I have never read it.'

'I assure you that you had no loss, as it's the most horrible nonsense imaginable. All that there's in it is an old man's playing at see-saw and learning Latin!'

The critique was cut short as they arrived at Mrs. Thorpe's lodgings. Mr. Thorpe immediately became the

dutiful and affectionate son. 'Ah, Mother! How do you do?' He said, shaking her heartily by the hand. 'Where did you get that quiz of a hat? It makes you look like an old witch. Morland and I have arrived to stay with you for a couple of days, so you must look out for a couple of beds somewhere nearby.'

Mrs. Thorpe received her son delightedly and affectionately. Then, John Thorpe bestowed his fraternal attention on his other two younger sisters, asking each of them how they did, and observing that both of them looked rather ugly. Catherine was not pleased by these manners; but he was James's friend and Isabella's brother; and her judgement was further soothed when Isabella assured her later that John perceived her to be the most charming girl in the world. Had Catherine been older, perhaps she would not have been affected by these sort of compliments. But when timidity and youth are united, it needs uncharacteristic steadiness of reason to resist the attraction of being addressed as the most charming girl in the world. So, when James asked her later when they were alone how she liked his friend John, she said,

'I like him very much; he seems very agreeable,' when she actually wanted to say, 'I do not like him at all.'

'He's as good-natured a fellow that ever was; a bit of a rattle perhaps; but I believe that will recommend him to your sex. How do you like the rest of the family?'

'Very much indeed, Isabella in particular.'

'I am very glad to hear you say that, as she is just the kind of young woman I would like to see you attached to. She has so much good sense and is so unaffected and amiable that I have always wished for you to know her. She seems fond of you as well and praised you to the skies. Even you must be proud of such praise from a girl like Miss Thorpe,' he said, taking her hand affectionately.

'I am indeed,' Catherine replied. 'I love her a lot, and am delighted that you like her too. You barely mentioned about her when you wrote to me about your visit here.'

'Well, that was because I thought I'd see you sooner. I hope you will spend a lot of time in each other's company, while you are at Bath. She has such a superior understanding that she is the favourite of the family. How much she must be admired in a place like this, is it not?'

'Yes, Mr. Allen thinks she is the prettiest girl in Bath.'

'Well, I dare say I do not know any man who is a better judge of beauty than Mr. Allen. I am in no doubt that you are happy here, Catherine, having such a companion and friend like Isabella Thorpe. The Allens, I am sure are kind to you?'

'Yes, they are. I was never so happy before. It will be further delightful than ever. How good of you to come so far to see me!'

James accepted this compliment, and ensured his conscience accepted it too. 'Indeed, Catherine, I love you dearly,' he stated with perfect sincerity.

James dropped off his sister at Pulteney Street, where Mr. and Mrs. Allen welcomed him with great warmth. He was invited to dine with them, but a pre-engagement in Edgar's Buildings forced him to decline politely. After James left, Catherine was left to happily browse through the pages of *Udolpho*, lost from all worldly concerns of dressing and dinner.

Chapter Seven

The Dance

The party from Pulteney Street reached the Upper Rooms in good time, considering the fact that the Thorpes and James Morland had arrived just two minutes before them. The dancing commenced a few minutes after they had been seated. James had to wait, however, as John had visited the card-room to speak with a friend, and Isabella absolutely insisted that she would not join the set unless Catherine did so too.

Catherine accepted this kindness with gratitude, but was disappointed when Isabella changed her mind after just three minutes. After speaking with James on the other side, she declared to Catherine, 'My dear, I am afraid that I must leave you as your brother is simply impatient to

begin. I know you will not mind my leaving and I know John will be back in a moment. Then, you may easily find me out.'

Catherine was too good-natured to oppose this move and the couple rushed off. With the younger Miss Thorpes dancing as well, Catherine was left to the mercy of Mrs. Thorpe and Mrs. Allen and she remained between them.

Catherine was irritated when Mr. Thorpe did not reappear as expected, because she wished to dance, and also because she had to remain seated with many other young ladies because they lacked a partner to dance. But even though she was disgraced, not a murmur passed Catherine's lips. After ten minutes, she was roused from this state of humiliation by the arrival of not Mr. Thorpe, but Mr. Tilney. He was three yards away but did not see her. Catherine's smile and blush died as he walked away, speaking with a fashionable and beautiful young lady, who leant on his arm. Catherine instantly deduced her to be his sister, not even once considering the fact that he could be lost forever, by being married already. It had not ever entered her head that Mr. Tilney could possibly be

married. He had not behaved or spoken like the married men she was acquainted with; he had never mentioned a wife, although he had acknowledged a sister. Now, Catherine sat erect, her cheeks redder than normal.

The lady accompanying Mr. Tilney and his companion was an acquaintance of Mrs. Thorpe and she walked ahead of them. She stopped to speak with Mrs. Thorpe and her companions did so, too. Catherine caught Mr. Tilney's eye and received a smile of recognition. She returned it with pleasure and he came forward to speak with both her and Mrs. Allen.

'I am very happy to see you again, sir,' Catherine declared. 'I was afraid you'd left Bath.'

He said that he had left only for a week, the very morning after the day he had the pleasure of meeting her. Mrs. Allen spoke to Mr. Tilney after that but was interrupted by Mrs. Thorpe requesting her to move a bit to accommodate Mrs. Hughes and Miss Tilney with seats, for they were joining their party.

Mr. Tilney asked Catherine to dance with him and although it was a delightful proposition for Catherine,

she declined. If Thorpe, who arrived just a little while later, had come a minute earlier, he would have seen Catherine's pain. Thorpe spoke easily about keeping Catherine waiting which did not help things. Then he spoke incessantly about the dogs and the horses of the friend he had been talking to. Catherine could not spot Isabella as they were dancing in different sets. How she wished to point out Mr. Tilney to her!

Catherine was relieved when Mrs. Hughes asked her to keep Miss Tilney company. Mrs. Hughes returned to her party, and the two ladies got acquainted with each other. Catherine was interested in Miss Tilney because of her good breeding, charming appearance, and relation to Mr. Tilney. But Catherine found her arm gently taken by Isabella before the two dances were scarcely concluded. 'My dearest creature, I have got you at last. I have been looking for you. How could you come into this set, when you knew I was in the other? How wretched I have been without you.'

'But dear Isabella, how could I get at you? I could not even see where you were.'

'I told your brother the very same thing, but he did not believe me. He would not move an inch. Why are you men so lazy, Mr. Morland? I have been scolding him, Catherine.'

Catherine detached Isabella and pointed out Miss Tilney to her. 'That is Mr. Tilney's sister!'

'Good Heavens! You don't say so. What a delightful girl! I have never seen anything so beautiful. But where is her all-conquering brother? Point him out to me this instant. I'm dying to see him.'

When the orchestra struck up a fresh dance, Isabella refused to be led to the dance floor by James. Instead, she accompanied Catherine to their earlier place. John Thorpe was absent there and Catherine rushed off to where Mrs. Thorpe and Mrs. Allen were sitting in the hope of finding Mr. Tilney there and being asked for a dance.

'I hope you have had an agreeable partner, my dear,' Mrs. Thorpe said, anxious for praise of her own son.

'Very agreeable, madam.'

'John has charming spirits, doesn't he?'

'Did you meet Mr. Tilney, my dear?' Mrs. Allen enquired.

'No, where is he?'

'Well, he was with us just now. But he said he was tired of lounging about and decided to go and dance. I thought he would ask you if he met you.'

Catherine looked around and spotted Mr. Tilney leading a young woman to the dance.

'Ah, he's got a partner! I wish he had asked you,' Mrs. Allen remarked, adding after a short silence, 'He's a very agreeable young man.'

'Indeed he is,' Mrs. Thorpe declared. 'Although I'm his mother, I must say that there is not a more agreeable young man in the world.'

'I think she thought I was speaking about her son,' Mrs. Allen whispered to Catherine. Catherine was both disappointed and irritated and when John Thorpe arrived to ask her to dance, she declined politely saying she was tired. Catherine found the rest of the evening dull as well, as Mr. Tilney had left their party for tea at his partner's table.

Reaching home, Catherine slept off her disappointment for a straight nine hours, waking up

with fresh hopes and fresh schemes. What was foremost on her mind was to improve her acquaintance with Miss Tilney, and she decided to seek her at the Pump Room at one. But her plan was upset when two open carriages drew up at her door at half-past twelve. In the first there was a servant and her brother drove Isabella in the second. When John Thorpe came running up and urged her to hurry up, she was still confused.

'Have you forgotten our engagement? We had agreed to take a drive this morning!' John declared.

They got into their carriage and Catherine was delighted when it started travelling smoothly.

'Old Allen is rich as a Jew, isn't he?' John Thorpe broke the silence after a few minutes. 'Old Allen, the man you are living with,' he added, as Catherine couldn't understand him.

'Oh! Mr. Allen, you mean. Yes, I believe he is very rich.' 'No children at all?'

'No.'

'A good thing for his next heirs. He's your godfather, isn't he?'

'No.'

'But you are always with them.'

'Yes, always.'

'He seems to be a good, kind fellow though, and has lived very well. Does he drink his bottle a day now?'

'His bottle a day? Why would you think of such a thing? He is a very temperate man.'

'Lord help you! You women are always thinking of men being in liquor. Why, I am sure that if everyone were to drink their bottle a day, the world would not see half the disorders it sees now.'

'I cannot believe it.'

'It would save thousands. Our foggy climate needs help, after all.'

'It does give me the idea that all of you at Oxford drink a lot of more wine than I thought you did. However, I am sure James doesn't drink so much.'

Thorpe then went on and on about the superiority of his carriage and horse in all England and how he was the best coachman.

'Do you think that James's gig could break down?' Catherine asked him suddenly.

'Well, there is no sound piece of iron on it and the wheels have been worn out for ten years at least. It is the most devilish rickety vehicle I have ever seen. I would not travel two miles in it for fifty thousand pounds. Thank God we have a better gig.'

'Good Lord! Let us turn back, as they will suffer an accident if we don't tell them how unsafe it is.'

'They will only have a fall if it breaks down; and there is plenty of dirt so the fall will be good. Oh, curse it! The carriage is safe if one knows how to drive it.'

Catherine listened in amazement as the man was giving two versions of the same story. Moreover, she found him to be totally conceited and repulsive. Later, Catherine met Mrs. Allen, who told her that she had met Mrs. Thorpe at the Pump Room and spent some time with her. Later they had met Mrs. Hughes, Mr. Tilney and Miss Tilney near the Crescent.

'Mrs. Hughes spoke a lot about her family to me,' Mrs. Allen revealed.

'Did she tell you which part of Gloucestershire they come from?'

'Yes, but I do not remember now. They are good people, and very rich. Mrs. Tilney was a Miss Drummond and she and Mrs. Hughes were schoolfellows. Miss Drummond had a very large fortune and received twenty thousand pounds from her father after her marriage, as well as five hundred pounds to buy wedding clothes.'

'Are Mr. and Mrs. Tilney still in Bath?'

'I think they are, but I'm not certain. I have a notion that they are both dead; at least the mother is. Yes, I'm positive that Mrs. Tilney is not alive as Mrs. Hughes told me that Miss Tilney received her mother's beautiful set of pearls on her wedding day. Those were set aside for her when her mother died.'

'Is Mr. Tilney the only son?'

'I am not sure about that, my dear. I think so though and I know he is a very fine young man.'

Catherine did not make further enquiries as she felt that Mrs. Allen had no real intelligence to provide. She felt unfortunate that she had missed a meeting with Mr. and Miss Tilney. The drive with John Thorpe in comparison, had been rather disagreeable.

Chapter Eight

Thorpe Plays Dirty

The Allens, Thorpes and Morlands met in the evening at the theatre. Catherine and Isabella were seated together and Isabella could not help herself from chattering away. 'You look delightful, my dear Catherine. You really have done your hair in a heavenly style. Do you want to attract everybody? My brother is already in love with you and Mr. Tilney's return to Bath makes it plain that he's attached to you. My mother claims he's the most delightful man. You must introduce him to me. Is he here?'

'No, I can't see him anywhere.'

'That's horrid. Am I never to be introduced to him? Do you like my gown? You know something, I sometimes

get sick of Bath. Your brother and I agreed that it's good to stay here for a few weeks, but we prefer the country to any other place. It's ridiculous how our opinions match.'

The next morning, Catherine made up her mind to see Miss Tilney again. Catherine managed to get away from Isabella and James to approach Miss Tilney in the Pump Room, and the two spoke at length.

'How well your brother dances,' Catherine remarked rather artlessly at the end of their conversation. This amused and surprised Miss Tilney.

'Henry?' She smiled. 'Yes, he dances very well.'

'He must have thought it odd that I wasn't free to dance even though I was seated. But I had been engaged for the day to Mr. Thorpe. I was surprised to see Mr. Tilney again as I thought he'd left Bath.'

'When Henry had the pleasure of seeing you, he was in Bath only for a few days. He had come to obtain lodgings for us.'

'Was the lady who danced with him on Monday a Miss Smith?'

'Yes. She is an acquaintance of Mrs. Hughes.'

'Do you think she's pretty?'

'Not very.'

'Doesn't he come to the Pump Room?'

'Sometimes. But he preferred to ride with my father this morning.'

Mrs. Hughes had arrived to fetch Miss Tilney and they departed after ensuring that they would see each other at the cotillion ball the next day. Catherine went home happy and what she would wear to the ball was her main worry now.

On Thursday evening, Catherine attended the ball, determined to avoid the sight of Mr. Thorpe, lest he ask her to dance again. She fidgeted when John Thorpe approached her and pretended not to listen when he spoke to her. The cotillions got over and the country-dancing began, but there was no sight of the Tilneys. Catherine had given up when suddenly she was approached by none other than Mr. Tilney himself, who asked her to dance. She accepted happily.

But as soon as they had begun to dance, they were interrupted.

'Miss Morland!' John Thorpe addressed her from behind. 'What is the meaning of this? I thought you and I were supposed to dance together.'

'I wonder why you should think so, as you never asked me.'

'That's a good one, by Jove! I asked you as soon as I entered and would have asked you again. But as soon as I turned around, you disappeared. That was a cursed, shabby trick! I came only to dance with you and I thought you were engaged to me ever since Monday. I was telling all my acquaintances that I was going to dance with the prettiest girl in the room and here you are dancing with someone else.'

'They will never think of me after a description like that.'

'If they do not I shall kick them out of the rooms. Who is the chap you are dancing with?'

'Mr. Tilney.'

'I do not know him. But he's a good figure of a man. Does he want a horse? A friend of mine has a horse to sell that would suit anybody-only forty guineas.'

Mr. Thorpe kept talking incessantly, till a long string of passing ladies pushed him back. Catherine's partner approached her to say, 'Had he stayed with you half a minute longer, that gentleman would have undone my patience. He has no business of usurping the attention of my partner from me. We have entered into a contract of mutual agreeableness for an evening. I think the country-dance is an emblem of marriage. Fidelity and complaisance are the principal duties where both are concerned. The men who do not choose to dance or marry, have no business with the partners or wives of their neighbours.'

'But the two are very different things.'

'You think they cannot be compared?'

'Of course, not. People who marry can never part, and must keep house together. But people who dance together only stay together for half an hour.'

'Such is your definition of matrimony and dancing then. Considered like that, the resemblance is definitely not striking. But allow me to explain. In both, man has the advantage of choice and woman only the power

of refusal. In both, man and woman are engaged and belong to each other till its dissolution. In both, they bestow themselves to each other and cannot allow their attentions to wander somewhere else. You agree?'

'Yes, it sounds very well as you say it. But I still think they are different and I cannot look at both in the same light.'

'Well, there is definitely a difference in one respect. In marriage, the man is supposed to provide for the support of the woman, who is to keep the home agreeable to the man. But in dancing, the roles are interchanged as the agreeableness is expected from the man while the woman provides the fan and lavender water.'

'I never thought of that.'

'Am I to assume that the duties of dancing are not as strict as wished by your partner? If any gentleman spoke to you, nothing can be done to restrain you?'

'Mr. Thorpe is such a good friend of my brother's that I must speak to him if addressed. But there are hardly three young men in the room I am acquainted with.'

'Is that to be my only security? Alas!'

'I'm sure you can't have a better one. For if I don't know anyone, it's impossible for me to talk to them. Besides, I do not want to talk to anybody.'

'Now that is a security to make me proceed with courage. Do you find Bath as agreeable as before?'

'Yes, more so, indeed.'

'You shall soon be tired of it, say at the end of six weeks.'

'I do not think I shall be tired even after six months.'

'Bath has little variety when compared to London.'

'It's for other people to judge for themselves. But for me, living in a small village in the country can never find greater sameness there as here in Bath. There are a variety of amusements and things to be done here that are not available there.'

'Aren't you fond of the country?'

'Yes, I am. I have always lived happily there. But one day in the country is exactly like another.'

'But you spend your time more rationally in the country. Here, you are pursuing amusement all day long.'

'Well, I do not find much at home. There I can only

go and call on Mrs. Allen.'

'What a picture of intellectual poverty, to go and call only on Mrs. Allen,' an amused Mr. Tilney stated. 'However, you'll have a lot of experiences in Bath to talk about when you sink in that abyss again.'

'Yes, I shall never lack about something to talk about to Mrs. Allen or anyone else. I so wish Papa and Mamma and the rest of my family could join us too. One can never be tired of Bath!'

They went to dance after that and Catherine spotted a gentleman looking at her earnestly for some time. He was a rather handsome man, although past the bloom, and he still possessed the vigour of life. He spoke to Mr. Tilney in a familiar whisper and moved away.

'That gentleman knows your name now,' Mr. Tilney informed her. 'You have a right to know his. That's General Tilney, my father.'

'Oh!' Was Catherine's only reply. Her eyes followed the general with interest and admiration. 'What a handsome family they are!' She thought.

The next day at noon, a country walk had been

planned. But it started raining heavily since morning and the rain did not subside at noon. But at half-past twelve, the sky began to clear and a gleam of sunshine surprised Catherine. Ten minutes later, a bright afternoon was confirmed and a little later, two open carriages carrying Isabella, James and Mr. Thorpe arrived. 'They have come for me,' Catherine stated to Mrs. Allen. 'But I cannot go with them as Miss Tilney might yet call.'

'Make haste, Miss Morland,' John Thorpe shouted from the stairs, as he climbed up. 'We are going to Bristol. How do you do, Mrs. Allen?' He arrived and greeted Mrs. Allen.

'Isn't Bristol far away?' Catherine enquired. 'However, I cannot accompany you today as I'm expecting some friends any moment.'

'What do you mean?' Thorpe exclaimed, as the others demanded an explanation, too.

'I am expecting Miss Tilney and her brother to call on me to take a country walk,' Catherine explained.

'You speak of the man who you danced with last night, don't you?' Thorpe demanded.

'Yes.'

'Well, I saw him drive up the Lansdown Road, driving a pretty girl.'

'Did you?'

'Upon my soul, I did. I also heard Tilney mention to a man on horseback that they were going as far as Wick Rocks.'

A disappointed Catherine decided to accompany Mr. Thorpe and his party now. The carriage travelled in silence except that Thorpe spoke to his horse. As they entered Argyle Buildings, Catherine spotted Mr. Tilney and his sister walking down the street. They were looking back at her. 'Stop! Mr. Thorpe!' Catherine cried impatiently. 'There's Miss Tilney. How could you tell me that they were gone?'

But Thorpe refused to stop, cracking his whip harder and laughing.

'How could you deceive me, Mr. Thorpe?' Catherine demanded. 'They must think of me as strange and rude. I am rather vexed and I shall have no pleasure at Clifton, nor anywhere else.'

Thorpe defended himself saying he had never seen two men alike like that in his whole life. Catherine was very sad after the drive ended and only found comfort in seeing the wonders of Blaize Castle. On the drive back to Bath, Thorpe made insulting remarks about Catherine's brother being a miser and a fool not to have a personal gig. Catherine learnt from the footman after reaching home that a gentleman and a lady had called for her. When informed that she had gone out with Mr. Thorpe, the lady had asked if Catherine had left a message. On his saying no, they had left. What disappointed Catherine even more was that Isabella insisted that the Tilneys were to be blamed for this incident, and not her brother.

Chapter Nine

An Engagement

Catherine decided to call on Miss Tilney the next morning, but to her disappointment, she was informed that the latter was not at home. Catherine left mortified, sure that Miss Tilney was at home but did not wish to see her. At the bottom of the street, Catherine looked back to see Miss Tilney emerge from the door, accompanied by her father. Catherine left, angry at the incivility displayed. But she checked her resentment, thinking how much hurt her own behaviour might have caused, however unknowingly.

Catherine was so dejected that she almost decided not to go to the theatre that night. But it was a play that she wanted to see desperately and so she decided to go. She saw Mr. Tilney and his father in the opposite box and

he just bowed at her when he caught her eye. Not even a smile! Catherine was miserable indeed and was anxious to explain the cause of her disappearance to him.

After the play ended, Mr. Tilney made his way to her box and she apologised to him for her behaviour the other day. But she was surprised in turn when Mr. Tilney apologised, as they had been delayed to reach her place that evening. Catherine was much relieved and they parted with a promise to make that walk happen as soon as possible. Catherine was delighted when Thorpe mentioned that General Tilney had praised her. She couldn't have hoped for a better evening.

Meanwhile, Isabella and James spoke in private about the Clifton plan, which had been deferred. It was determined that they would leave the day after, and Catherine was confided in after Thorpe's assent was taken. But Catherine refused to go as she was determined now to keep her appointment with Miss Tilney regarding their appointed walk. Isabella tried to persuade Catherine in all possible ways and then tried another method. She reproached Catherine for having more affection for Miss

Tilney, although knowing her less than Isabella. Even Catherine's brother was greatly offended when she still refused. Thorpe then left them for a while and returned to state to Catherine, 'Well, I have settled the matter. I have been to Miss Tilney and made your excuses. I told her that you sent me to tell her that you were accompanying us to Clifton tomorrow because of a prior engagement, and would not have the pleasure of walking with her till Tuesday. She said yes to that, and that Tuesday would be as convenient to her.'

Isabella and James were happy but Catherine was not. 'I simply cannot submit to this,' she declared. 'Mr. Thorpe had no right to speak on my behalf. Because of Mr. Thorpe, I was led to being rude on Friday. I shall not make the same mistake again.'

Catherine then left them and made her way towards the Tilney residence. She informed the servant that she must speak to Miss Tilney at once and then hurried by him to reach upstairs. Catherine found herself in the drawing-room with General Tilney, her son, and her daughter. She explained her intrusion and was surprised to learn that

John Thorpe had indeed passed on the message. Miss Tilney had been surprised at it.

Catherine was received very warmly by the general and when she rose to take her leave after fifteen minutes, she was invited by the general to dine and spend the rest of the day with his daughter. Miss Tilney added her wishes and Catherine although honoured and happy, was forced to decline the offer as the Allens expected her back soon. The general hoped that she would be able to attend on a day when a longer notice could be given, and Catherine happily agreed, saying it would be her pleasure.

The next morning, the Tilneys did call on the appointed time. The heroine took a walk with the hero himself, around the beautiful hill called Beechen Cliff. 'It reminds me of the south of France,' Catherine observed. 'You've been abroad, then?' A surprised Henry asked. 'No. I meant what I had read about in *The Mysteries of Udolpho*. But you don't read novels, do you?'

'Why not?'

'Well, gentlemen think they are not clever enough for them. They prefer better books.'

'The person, gentleman or lady, who has not derived pleasure in reading a novel, must be intolerably stupid. I have read all of Mrs. Radcliffe's works and enjoyed most of them. *The Mysteries of Udolpho* was something I couldn't put down till I had finished it. I recall finishing it in two days.'

'Yes,' Miss Tilney recalled. 'I remember you reading it aloud to me.'

Although Catherine shared Miss Tilney's fondness of literature and history, she was quite at sea when the Tilneys viewed the country like artists. She knew nothing about drawing and art, and was ashamed of her ignorance. Catherine confessed about her lack of knowledge, and Henry Tilney gave her a talk on foregrounds, distances, and second distances- side-screens and perspectives- lights and shades; and Catherine listened in rapt attention, pleasing the speaker. The walk ended with the Tilneys escorting Catherine home and Miss Tilney requested of Mrs. Allen the pleasure of Catherine's company to dinner the day after the next.

The next day, a note from Isabella arrived, seeking peace and reconciliation. Catherine was summoned by her on a matter of utmost importance, and she reached her friend's place. Isabella embraced Catherine warmly and gave her the happy news that she was engaged to her brother! Catherine was just as happy as Isabella and the two ladies hugged, shedding tears of joy. Isabella's entire family was happy at this alliance. When James wrote to say that his parents had agreed to the alliance, their joy was doubled. John Thorpe prepared to depart for London, as he had only been waiting for the letter to arrive. He came to say goodbye to Catherine in the parlour. They parted after John Thorpe asked her if she would mind if he visited her at Fullerton and she gave her assent saying that her family would be pleased with his visit.

'I hope you will not be sorry to see me, Miss Morland.'

'Oh dear, not all. Company is always cheerful.'

Chapter Ten

Captain Tilney

Catherine had such great expectations of her visit to the Tilney residence that her disappointment was but inevitable. Although she was welcomed warmly by the General and his daughter, and although Henry was at home, there was a lack of intimacy on Miss Tilney's part. Henry spoke little, and was not as agreeable as before. It couldn't be General Tilney's fault as he was perfectly good-natured and kind. How could he be blamed for the lack of spirit in his children?

When she returned, Isabella termed this behaviour as the haughtiness and pride of the Tilneys. How could they treat their guest with such superciliousness, by barely speaking with her?

'It wasn't as bad at that, Isabella; there was no superciliousness; she was very civil,' Catherine protested.

'Oh Catherine! Don't defend her. How could her brother behave so, being so attached to you? It is impossible to discern the feelings of some people. So, he hardly looked at you the entire day?'

'I did not say so; but he did not seem to be in good spirits.'

'How contemptible! I'm averse to inconsistency above all things. Do not think of him again, dear Catherine. He seems unworthy of you.'

'Unworthy? I do not suppose he ever thinks of me.'

'Yes, that is what I think too. How different than your brother and mine. I do believe John has the most constant heart.'

'Well, let us see how they behave at the rooms this evening.'

'Must I go?'

'You do not intend to? I thought it was planned.'

'No, but I can't refuse you anything. But do not insist on my being too agreeable, as my heart will be forty miles away. I beg you not to mention dancing, as it is simply out

of the question. Charles Hodge will plague me to death, as he guesses the reason. But I shall cut him short.'

Isabella's opinion of the Tilneys did not influence Catherine, who was sure that they held no pride in their hearts. Her confidence was rewarded that evening, when she was greeted with the same kindness and affection as before, by the Tilneys. Miss Tilney took pains to give her company, and Henry asked her to dance. Catherine had heard the day before that their elder brother, Captain Tilney, was due to arrive. So when she spotted a fashionable, handsome young man in their party, she immediately guessed who he was. Catherine looked at him admiringly, thinking that some people might consider him handsomer than his younger brother, although to her his air was more assuming, and his countenance less prepossessing.

He was also not very tasteful, and lacked manners as he had loudly protested against dancing himself, and had even laughed at Henry for doing so. Catherine enjoyed her usual dance with Henry, and was finding him irresistible, when the unthinkable happened at the end of the first dance. Captain Tilney pulled his brother

away and they left whispering together. Catherine was naturally uneasy, and this feeling lasted for fifteen long minutes, before the two returned. The explanation for this unusual behaviour was provided by Henry, requesting Catherine if Miss Thorpe would be willing to dance, as his brother would be happy to be introduced to her. Catherine immediately replied that she was sure Miss Thorpe did not intend to dance at all. Captain Tilney received the cruel reply and walked away.

'I know your brother won't mind it, as I heard him say before that he detests dancing,' Catherine stated. 'It was good-natured for him to ask, as I think he saw Isabella seated, and thought she longed for a partner. But he is mistaken, as she would not dance on any account.'

'How easily you understand the motive of other people's actions,' Henry smiled and stated.

'What do you mean?'

'Should I? I'm afraid the consequences will greatly embarrass you, and form a disagreement between us.'

'No, it shall not do either. I'm not afraid.'

'Well then, all I meant that attributing my brother's

wish to dance with Miss Thorpe to good nature, makes me convinced that you are the most good-natured person in this world.'

Catherine blushed, but something in his words confused her. After a while, she was surprised to see Isabella agree to dance with Captain Tilney. Isabella caught her eye, shrugged and smiled.

'I do not know how this happened,' an astonished Catherine said to her partner. 'Isabella was so determined not to dance.'

'Did Isabella never change her mind before this?'

'But how could your brother ask her after what he heard from you?'

'I am not surprised on that account. You ask me to be surprised on your friend's account, so I am; but my brother's conduct is something I rather expected. The beauty of your friend was an open attraction, and only you can comprehend her firmness.'

'You laugh, but I assure you that Isabella is very firm in general.'

'The same can be said of anyone. To always be firm is to always be obstinate. I do think Miss Thorpe hasn't chosen badly.'

After the dancing was over, Isabella explained to Catherine, 'I refused him for as long as I could, but he wouldn't take no for an answer. You have no idea how he pressed me. I pleaded with him to get another partner, but he spoke nonsense like there was no one else in the room he wanted to be with other than me. I realised I would have no peace unless I agreed. Besides, Mrs. Hughes introduced us and she would have thought ill if I did not agree. I am so glad it's over!'

'He is a handsome man!'

'Yes, I suppose he is. But he is not in my style of beauty. I hate dark eyes and a florid complexion in a man. He's also extremely conceited. I took him down many times, in my way.'

When the young ladies met next, they had a better topic to discuss. James Morland's second letter had come in, where his father's kind intentions were explained. A living of the value of four hundred pounds annually was to be given to his son when he was old enough to receive it. An estate of equal value was assured as his future inheritance. James also expressed the desire to wait for two to three years before they could marry. Catherine was

equally satisfied, and heartily congratulated Isabella for being so well settled in life.

'It is very charming,' Isabella said gravely. 'Mr. Morland has behaved handsomely, indeed.'

'I only wish I could do as much,' Mrs. Thorpe stated, looking anxiously at her daughter. 'One cannot expect more of him, although four hundred a year is a small income to begin on. But dear Isabella, your wishes are so moderate.'

'I do not seek more on my account, but I cannot bear to see my dear Morland injured. I cannot make him sit on an income barely enough to meet the necessities of life. I never think of myself.'

'I know you never do, my dear. But let us not distress Catherine by talking about such things,' Mrs. Thorpe stated.

'No one can think better of Mr. Morland than I do. But everyone has their failing, and a right to do what they want with their money.'

Catherine was hurt by these statements, and declared, 'I am very sure that my father has promised to do as much as he can afford.'

Isabella recollected herself immediately. 'There cannot be a doubt about that, dear Catherine. You know me well enough to be sure that I would be satisfied with a smaller income. It's not the lack of money that makes me dispirited. I hate money. It's the sting of waiting for those endless two and a half years, before your brother can hold the living.'

Catherine's uncomfortable feelings lessened, as she believed that the delay of the marriage was the sole cause of Isabella's distress. Isabella was cheerful when she saw her again, and when James arrived, he was received with great kindness.

Chapter Eleven

Isabella Behaves Strangely

The Allens were now on their sixth week in Bath, and Catherine waited with a beating heart, as it was only natural that the time to depart was near. For her acquaintance with the Tilneys to end so suddenly was an evil she could not come to terms with. It was then that General Tilney made Catherine a rather generous proposal. He invited Catherine to Northanger Abbey in Gloucestershire, as a companion for Miss Tilney. Catherine was ecstatic at this invitation, and requested that she obtain her parents' permission. She wrote home, and the consent was easily granted.

Catherine was equally excited to be close to Henry as well as Northanger Abbey. Her historical interests were aroused, as Northanger Abbey had been a richly endowed

convent at the time of the Reformation, having fallen into the possession of an ancestor of the Tilneys after its dissolution. A large portion of the ancient building made up for the present dwelling, while the rest was decayed. Northanger Abbey stood low in a valley, protected from the north and east by rising oak woods.

Catherine was so happy that two or three days passed by without her seeing Isabella for more than a few minutes. She realised this and longed to converse with her, when she pulled Catherine aside in the Pump Room one day.

'I am so happy you are going to Northanger! It is one of the finest old places in England after all. Well, I've just received a letter from John. He is head over heels in love with you!'

'With me, Isabella?'

'My dearest Catherine, modesty is quite well, but this is being absurd. You are fishing for compliments! He said in his letter that you received his advances kindly, and now he wants me to urge his suit, and say all pretty things to you.'

Catherine expressed her astonishment at this declaration and denied any knowledge of Mr. Thorpe's

being in love with her. She also denied encouraging his advances. Isabella was silent.

'Do not be angry with me, my dearest Isabella. I shall never speak disrespectfully of your brother. I know he is not the one for me. But we shall still remain sisters.'

'Well, John wished I should speak with you on the matter, and I have. I must admit I found the idea foolish once it was suggested. I would never want you to sacrifice your happiness just to oblige me and my brother. Why should a brother's happiness mean more to me than a friend's? Ah! There he comes. But I'm sure he shall not see us.'

Catherine saw Captain Tilney enter, and Isabella staring at him, soon caught his eye. He immediately took the seat where Isabella's movements invited him.

'What! Always to be watched, in person or by proxy!' He stated, and Catherine started.

'Nonsense!' Isabella whispered. 'Why do you put such thoughts into my head? I possess an independent spirit.'

'I wish your heart were independent. That would be enough for me.'

'My heart, indeed! What do you have to do with

hearts? None of you men have any hearts.'

'If not hearts, we have eyes; and they torment us enough.'

'I am sorry they do. I'm sorry they find something disagreeable in me. I will look the other way. Hope that pleases you, and your eyes are not tormented now.'

'Moreover so, as the edge of a blooming cheek is still in view- too much and yet, too little!'

Catherine stood up, amazed that Isabella could endure this, and feeling jealous for her brother. She proposed that they should join Mrs. Allen, but Isabella displayed no inclination of doing so. She told Catherine that she was tired, and was expecting her sisters. But Catherine could be equally stubborn, and she walked out of the Pump Room, leaving Isabella and Captain Tilney together. She left them with great uneasiness, as it seemed to her that Captain Tilney was in love with Isabella, who was encouraging him. Catherine wished to warn Isabella, both for her sake as well as her own brother's sake. But Isabella had displayed thoughtlessness when she tried to propagate John Thorpe's affection for Catherine. In the next few days, Catherine kept a close watch on her friend, and what she saw was not agreeable. She saw Isabella acknowledge Captain Tilney's attentions readily

in public, and James suffered because of it. Catherine saw him serious and uneasy. The name of Captain Tilney seemed a passport to Isabella's goodwill.

When Catherine learnt that Captain Tilney had no intention of accompanying them to Gloucestershire, and preferred to remain in Bath, she decided to speak to Henry. She asked him to persuade his elder brother to leave Bath.

'I cannot persuade someone like him,' he replied. 'I have told him that Miss Thorpe is engaged.'

'He does not know the pain he is giving my brother!'

'Is it my brother's attentions to Miss Thorpe, or her attention to him that causes the pain?'

'Isn't it the same thing?'

'I think Mr. Morland would see the difference. No man is offended by another man's interest in the woman he loves. It is the woman's interest that causes the pain.'

'Isabella is wrong. But I'm sure she means no harm, as she has been in love with my brother since they first met.'

'I understand perfectly. She is in love with James, and flirts with Frederick.'

'A woman in love with one man cannot flirt with another.'

'Well, it is probable that she will neither love nor flirt well. The gentlemen must each give up a little.'

'Is your father comfortable about Captain Tilney staying? Surely, if he asked him, he would leave.'

'Miss Morland, don't you think you are getting carried away too far on account of securing your brother's comfort? Do you think he would thank you that Miss Thorpe's good behaviour can be guaranteed by not seeing Captain Tilney? If you do not doubt the mutual attachment between your brother and Miss Thorpe, be assured that no jealousy can be aroused there. Frederick will stay here for only a short time, perhaps a few days more than us. He must return to his regiment, as his leave of absence will soon end. Miss Thorpe will laugh with your brother over poor Captain Tilney's passion for a month.'

Chapter Twelve

Northanger Abbey

Isabella was sad to part from Catherine, just as the Allens. The journey from Bath to Northanger began and Catherine was surprised when the general asked her to take his place in his son's curricle. He wanted her to see as much of the country as possible. Henry was such a good driver that he impressed Catherine. He drove well, and he drove quietly, without swearing at the horses or whipping them. He was so different from the only other gentleman-coachman that she had encountered! Next to dancing with him, being driven by him was certainly the greatest happiness in Catherine's world.

Henry thanked Catherine for agreeing to be his sister's companion as Eleanor had no friends.

'But are you not with her?' She asked.

'Northanger is half my home. I have an establishment at my own house in Woodston, twenty miles away. Some of my time is spent there.'

'How sorry you must be because of that!'

'I am always sorry to leave Eleanor.'

'Yes, but you must also be fond of the abbey! After being used to such a home, surely an ordinary parsonage-house must be disagreeable.'

'You seemed to have formed a very favourable impression of the abbey,' he smiled and stated.

'Of course I have. Isn't it a fine old place, like what one reads about?'

'And are you prepared to meet all the horrors that a building like that is capable of producing? Do you possess a strong heart?'

'Oh! Yes- I do not think I can be easily frightened. Besides, there would be so many people in the house, and it hasn't been left uninhabited for years after all.'

'Yes, of course we don't have to explore our way into

a hall dimly lit by a wood fire. Nor do we have to sleep in a room without doors, windows or furniture. But you must be knowing that when a young lady is introduced to this kind of house, she is always lodged apart from the rest of the family. The ancient housekeeper, Dorothy, escorts her up a different staircase, along many gloomy passages, into an apartment unused for about twenty years, since a cousin or kin died in it. Can you stand such a ceremony? Won't your heart sink?'

'Oh, but I am sure this won't happen to me.'

'Dorothy, in the meanwhile, tells you that the house is haunted. Then, she leaves, and when her footsteps recede, you try to fasten the door, only to realise that it has no lock!'

'How frightful, Mr. Tilney! This is just like a book! But I'm sure this can't happen to me. I'm also sure that your housekeeper is not named Dorothy. Well, what next?'

'Nothing further alarming may occur on the first night. But on the second, and the third night after your

arrival, you will probably experience a violent storm. Thunder so loud that the very foundations of the house will shake, along with the gusts of wind that accompany it. You will rise and put on your dressing-gown, eager to examine this mystery. You will discover a hidden door, and pass through it, lamp in hand, to a small vaulted room.

'No! I shall be too frightened to do such thing.'

'What? Not when Dorothy has let you in the secret that there is a secret tunnel between your apartment and the Chapel of St Anthony, barely two miles away? Can you resist such an adventure? No indeed! You will proceed into this vaulted room that will lead to several others. One might have a dagger, another a few drops of blood, and an instrument of torture might exist in the third. But as your lamp is almost exhausted, you shall return to your apartment. But while crossing the small vaulted room, your eyes will fall upon a large, old-fashioned cabinet of ebony and gold. You will discover nothing after searching in it, except a considerable hoard

of diamonds. Finally, after touching a secret spring, an inner compartment will be revealed. A roll of paper will lie here, containing many sheets of manuscript. You rush to your room with the treasure, but your lamp is suddenly extinguished just as you are about to read it, leaving you in total darkness.'

'Oh no! Well, go on!'

But Henry was much too amused now to carry it further. Catherine was ashamed of her eagerness now, and began telling him that she was sure that Miss Tilney would not subject her to such tortures, and that she was not at all afraid. As they almost reached the end of their journey, Catherine grew impatient for her first sight of the abbey. But as they reached, a sudden burst of rain prevented Catherine from getting a good view. She was quickly escorted from the carriage to the shelter of the old porch, and reached the hall, where the general welcomed her. As Catherine entered the common drawing room, she thought that it was really delightful to be in an abbey! But the furniture though elegant, was modern. The windows

were not preserved in their true Gothic form; true, the pointed arch had been preserved, but each pane was large, clear and light!

The general spoke about the furniture for some time, and then surprisingly declared that it was twenty minutes of five! This seemed to hint at separation, as Miss Tilney guided Catherine away. Catherine realised that the strictest punctuality of family hours was expected at Northanger. They returned to the large hall and ascended a broad, shining oak staircase. After many flights and landing places, they arrived at a long, wide gallery. It had a range of doors on one side, and was lighted on the other side by windows that looked out into a quadrangle. Miss Tilney led the way into a chamber, and left quickly.

Chapter Thirteen

The Storm

Catherine realised instantly that her apartment was very dissimilar to the one Henry had alarmed her with his description. It was not large and had neither tapestry nor velvet. The walls were papered and the floor, carpeted. The furniture was handsome and comfortable, and the room looked cheerful. Her heart at ease, Catherine went about examining the contents of the room. Her eye suddenly fell on a large high chest on one side of the fireplace. She stared at it in wonder.

Catherine moved forward and examined the chest. It was of cedar but laid with some darker wood, and raised about a foot from the ground on a carved stand. It had an old silver lock and broken silver handles. The centre

of the lid had a mysterious cipher in the same metal. She raised the lid with great difficulty. But a sudden knocking at the door made her drop the lid, which closed violently.

Miss Tilney's maid was the intruder, who had been sent by her to be of use to Miss Morland. Catherine dismissed her immediately, anxious to investigate the mystery. With a great effort, she threw back the lid, and saw with astonished eyes a white cotton counterpane, neatly folded, resting at one end of the chest. Miss Tilney entered suddenly, anxious that Catherine get ready.

'That is a curious old chest, is it not?' Miss Tilney said, as an embarrassed Catherine hastily closed it. 'It's impossible to say how many generations it has been here. I do not know when it was first put here, but I did not have it moved as I thought it might be useful to store hats and bonnets. Its weight makes it difficult to open though, so it's better off in that far corner.'

Catherine blushed in reply, and Miss Tilney hinted at being late.

In half a minute, they ran downstairs together. This haste was justified, as General Tilney was pacing the

drawing room, watch in hand. He pulled the bell violently as soon as they entered.

'Dinner to be on the table directly!' He ordered. Catherine shook at this manner, but the general was soon back to his polite ways, scolding his daughter for hurrying her fair friend so foolishly. After dinner, Catherine retired to her apartment.

The night was a stormy one, with the wind rising throughout the afternoon. It was violent when the party broke up after dinner. Just as Catherine was about to get into bed, she saw a high, old-fashioned black cabinet she hadn't noticed before. She recalled Henry's description of the ebony cabinet, and it was a remarkable coincidence. She could not sleep till she had examined it, but it resisted all her strength. She relentlessly tried opening the cabinet with the key, till it suddenly opened. She saw a double range of small drawers, with larger ones above and below after throwing open each folding door. She opened four drawers but each was empty! After some time, only the place in the middle was left unexplored. After managing to open the same with equal difficulty, she saw a roll of

paper pushed back deep inside, clearly for concealment. Catherine's heart fluttered as she gripped the manuscript. Catherine saw her candle light dim, and inspected it with alarm. It still had some hours to burn. She hastily snuffed it. Alas! It was snuffed and extinguished in one. Catherine was struck with horror as darkness engulfed the room. A sudden gust of wind added to the terror.

As Catherine trembled all over, she heard receding footsteps, and the closing of a distant door. The manuscript fell from her hand as she groped her way towards bed and clambered in. The storm raged dreadfully. The strange sounds she heard seemed more horrific than the wind; the curtains of her bed seemed to be in motion, the lock of her door was agitated as if someone was trying to enter, murmurs along the gallery and distant moans!

Hour after hour went by, till Catherine heard all the clocks in the house strike three, before the tempest subsided or she fell into deep sleep unknowingly.

Chapter Fourteen

The Mystery of Mrs. Tilney

Catherine woke up when the housemaid folded back her window shutters at eight o' clock. Recollecting the manuscript, she quickly picked up all the scattered pages from the ground and rushed back to her bed to study them. But could it be possible, or were her eyes playing strange tricks on her? An inventory of linen was all that was before her! The second, third, fourth, and fifth were no different. Two others, penned by the same hand, featured an expenditure note. The larger sheet was a ferrier's bill!

Catherine felt silly and humbled that such absurd fancies had robbed her night's sleep. How could she have brought this upon herself? Heaven forbid that Henry Tilney got to know about this! In a way, it was his own doing, as if the cabinet hadn't matched his description,

she wouldn't have been slightly curious about it. She returned the papers to the cabinet hastily, unwilling to retain any evidence of her folly.

Catherine rushed to the breakfast parlour, where Henry was alone. She spoke naturally to him, anxious not to have her folly discovered. The general joined them soon, and Henry left for Woodston after breakfast. Business would keep him there for two or three days. The general displayed the abbey to Catherine from the lawn, and she was awestruck and full of praise for it. The entire building enclosed a large court; and two sides of the quadrangle were luxuriously draped in Gothic ornaments. Knolls of old trees surrounded the remainder, and beautiful steep woody hills rose behind.

The kitchen garden was next in display, and the number of acres here were double of all that Mr. Allen and her father possessed, including churchyard and orchard. The walls appeared endless and countless; a village of hothouses almost rose from them with an entire parish at work within the enclosure. After the general had given an exhaustive tour, it was time to return. 'Why do you choose that cold, damp path, Eleanor?' He demanded. 'Our best way is across the park.'

'This is such a favourite walk of mine that I always think it to be the nearest and best. Maybe it is damp.'

It was a narrow, winding path through a thick grove of old Scotch firs. It looked so gloomy that Catherine was eager to enter it. The general excused himself on account of the rays of the sun, and took the other way. Catherine realised she was relieved that he had left.

'I'm particularly fond of this spot, as it was my mother's favourite walk,' Miss Tilney confessed. This was the first time Catherine had heard Mrs. Tilney being mentioned. She listened attentively for more. 'I used to walk here often with her,' Eleanor added. 'I didn't love it as much then as I do now, though. Her memory endears it now.'

'It does not endear it to her husband,' Catherine reflected. 'The general wouldn't enter it.'

As Eleanor was silent, she added, 'Her death must have been a great affliction.'

'A great and increasing one,' Eleanor replied, in a low voice. 'I was only thirteen when it happened. Although I felt the loss rather strongly then, I did not, could not comprehend what a great loss it was. I have no sister, and although Henry is an extremely affectionate brother, which I'm most thankful for, it is impossible for

me not to be solitary mostly.'

'You must miss her a lot.'

'A mother should be always present. She would have been a constant friend, and her influence would have exceeded that of all others.'

'Was she a handsome woman? Charming? Do you have any pictures of her in the abbey? Why was she so partial to the grove?' These questions poured forth now, and Miss Tilney answered the first three questions, passing by two others.

Catherine's interest in the deceased Mrs. Tilney grew, and she was sure that Mrs. Tilney had been unhappy in marriage, and that the general had been an unkind husband. How could he have loved her if he did not love her walk?

'I suppose her picture hangs in your father's room?' Catherine enquired.

'No; it was intended for the drawing room; but my father was not satisfied with the painting, and it had no place for a while. I took it after her death, and hung it in my bedchamber. I shall be happy to show it to you.'

Here was yet another proof. The portrait of a deceased wife, not valued by the husband! He must have

been exceedingly cruel to her!

The feelings Catherine felt for the general amounted to aversion now. She had often read about such characters, but now had experienced one in real life. The end of the path brought them again to the general, and Catherine was obliged to walk with him again. She was forced to listen to him, and to smile when he did. But she was withdrawn, and this was noticed and perceived to be ill-health by the general. He ordered his daughter to return home with her, where he would join them shortly. Eleanor was strictly ordered not to take her friend round the abbey till he returned. Catherine thought this was remarkable as he wished to delay what she wanted.

The general arrived only after an hour, and after being coaxed by his daughter, gave Catherine a guided tour of the house. The real drawing room was magnificent in both size and furniture. The library was equally magnificent, with an impressive collection of books. Returning to the hall, they ascended the chief staircase to proceed in the opposite direction from the gallery where Catherine's room was. They soon entered another planned the same way, but superior in length and breadth. Three large bed chambers were displayed here

that seemed equipped for royalty. Folding doors ended this gallery that Miss Tilney had now thrown open. She had passed through and was almost about to enter the first door to the left that led to another long gallery, when the general stopped her hastily. He demanded angrily where she was going. What else remained to be seen? Hadn't Miss Morland seen whatever was meant to be seen?

Miss Tilney drew back, and the doors were shut upon Catherine. A momentary glance had revealed to her a narrower passage, numerous openings, and a winding staircase. Catherine wanted to examine this part of the house now more than anything else. The general's prevention was an additional stimulant and she was sure that something was concealed here. Miss Tilney's short sentence as they followed the general downstairs, seemed to explain the general's behaviour.

'I was about to take you into what was my mother's room; the room in which she died.'

When she was alone with Eleanor, Catherine expressed her desire to see the room, and was promised to be taken at a convenient hour.

'How long has it been since your mother died?'

'Nine years.'

'Were you there to the last?'

'No,' Miss Tilney sighed. 'I was away from home, unfortunately. Her illness was short and sudden, and she was gone before I arrived.'

Catherine's blood ran cold as her mind was full of horrid suggestions. Was it possible that Henry's father…? There were so many examples to justify the blackest of suspicions. She saw him in the evening again, pacing the drawing room for an hour in silent thoughtfulness, with eyes downcast and contracted brow. Could it be that his past sense of guilt was haunting him? Miss Tilney caught her looking at her father repeatedly. 'It is not unusual for my father to walk about the room in this way,' she whispered.

Catherine was glad to be dismissed, as the general stated that he had many pamphlets to finish before he retired. This was not likely, Catherine thought. Surely, something else kept him awake rather than stupid pamphlets. Something that could only be done while the others slept.

Chapter Fifteen

A Sense of Shame

The next day did not provide an opportunity for Catherine to examine the mysterious apartments. It was a busy day being Sunday, and her courage did not permit exploring the same after dinner. The next morning was promising, and during the general's early walk, Catherine asked Miss Tilney to fulfill her promise. The latter agreed, but Catherine wished to see the portrait in her bedchamber first. The portrait represented a rather lovely woman, with a mild and pensive countenance.

Eleanor and Catherine entered the great gallery after that. But they spotted the dreaded figure of the general at the end of the gallery. His cry of 'Eleanor' resonated loudly throughout the building, as she rushed to join him. They disappeared together, and Catherine fled to

the safety of her room. She remained there fearfully for an hour, hoping to be summoned by the general anytime.

But she was not called and she decided to descend when she saw a carriage arrive. It was best to meet the general under protection of visitors. The breakfast room was crowded and she was introduced by the general as the friend of his daughter, which concealed his anger well.

Catherine decided that she would make an attempt on the forbidden door alone. It would be better if Eleanor did not know about the matter, as it was not fair for her to take the blame. At four o' clock, Catherine reached the gallery alone. She silently slipped through the folding doors and reached the door to enter. The apartment was large and well-proportioned, with a large bed. There was a bright Bath stove, mahogany wardrobes and neatly painted chairs. A sense of shame came over Catherine as she realised she had been mistaken. She longed to retire to her room as being discovered here by a servant would be unpleasant, and much worse, by the general himself. Catherine closed the door and exited. Instantly, a door underneath was quickly opened and someone ascended the stairs swiftly. Catherine was like a statue as she stared at the staircase. 'Mr. Tilney!' She exclaimed in astonishment. Henry was astonished too. 'How come you came up that staircase?' She said. 'Why shouldn't I?' He asked in surprise. 'It is the nearest way from the stable yard to my own chamber.'

Catherine blushed deeply. 'May I ask how you came here?' He asked.

'I came to see your mother's room.'

'My mother's room? Is there anything extraordinary to be seen there?'

'Nothing at all. I thought you wouldn't return till tomorrow.'

'I had nothing to detain me further. You look pale! I'm afraid my running so fast upon the stairs has alarmed you.'

'You've had a fine day for a ride.'

'Very; does Eleanor leave you to find your way into all the rooms in the house all by yourself?'

'Oh! No; she showed me the most on Saturday. We were coming to these rooms, but your father was with us,' she said, dropping her voice. 'That prevented you?' Henry stated, looking at her earnestly. 'Have you looked into all the rooms there?'

'No, I just wanted to see…Is it not late? I must go and dress.'

'It's only a quarter past four. You are not in Bath now. There are no theatre or rooms to prepare for. In Northanger, half an hour is enough.'

'Have you received any letter from Bath since I saw you last?' He asked, as they walked slowly up the gallery.

'No. I'm surprised as Isabella promised to write faithfully.'

'A faithful promise! That is puzzling. The fidelity of promising is little worth knowing, as it can deceive and pain you. My mother's room is wonderful, is it not? It is the most comfortable apartment in the house, and I've always wondered why Eleanor doesn't take it for her own. Did she send you to look at it?'

'No.'

'So it's your own doing entirely?'

Catherine was silent, and he added, 'Since there is nothing curious about the room, this must have come from a sentiment of respect for my mother's character. I believe the world hasn't seen a better woman. I suppose Eleanor has spoken a lot about her.'

'Yes. I mean, not much. But what she said was very interesting. Her sudden death, and none of you being at home. Your father, I thought, perhaps had not been too fond of her.'

'So you infer the probability of some negligence?'

Catherine shook her head.

'Or maybe something less pardonable?'

Catherine looked at him straight in the eye, and he continued. 'The illness, the seizure that took my mother's life, was sudden. The constitutional cause was the bilious fever she often suffered from. A physician attended her on the third day, a very respectable man, in whom she had always placed great confidence. When he mentioned the danger, two more physicians were summoned the very next day, who constantly attended her for twenty–four hours. She died on the fifth day. Both Frederick and I were at home then, and attended her repeatedly. All possible attentions were bestowed on our mother. Poor Eleanor was absent, and returned only to see her mother in a coffin.'

'Was your father afflicted?'

'Greatly so, for a time. You are wrong to assume that he was not attached to her. He loved her as much as it was possible for him to. All of us do not possess the same tenderness of disposition. But although his temper injured her, his judgement never did. He valued her sincerely, and was truly afflicted by her death, if not permanently.'

'I am glad to hear that. It would have been very shocking!'

'You have formed such a surmise of horror that I cannot even utter. What is the basis of your judgement? Remember the country and age we live in. Remember we are English, and Christians. Does our education prepare us for such atrocities? In a country where social and literary intercourse is on such a footing, and where newspapers lay everything open, is something like this possible? What ideas have you been admitting, Miss Morland?'

They had reached the end of the gallery, and Catherine ran off to her room with tears of shame.

Chapter Sixteen

A Trip to Woodston

Catherine's visions of romance had ended! Henry's short address had opened her eyes to her extravagant fancies. Humbled, she cried bitterly. Her folly was now exposed to him, and he must hate her forever. She hated herself more than ever. She could barely reply to Eleanor's query if she was well, when she descended at five. Henry joined them soon, and paid her more attention than usual. It seemed that he was aware that Catherine needed comfort.

Catherine made up her mind to judge and act in the future with the greatest good sense. Her heart longed to hear from Isabella, who had broken her promise to write. It seemed so strange! For nine mornings she waited for a letter, and on the tenth day, Henry handed her a letter. It was from James, and said:

Dear Catherine,

God knows I have little inclination for writing. But it is my duty to tell you that everything between me and Miss Thorpe has come to an end. I left her and Bath yesterday, never to see either again. I shall not enter into particulars, as they will pain you even more. You will soon know where the blame lies; and I hope you will forgive your brother of everything but the folly of thinking that his affection was returned. Thank God I'm undeceived in time! But it is a heavy blow! That too, after father's consent was given. But no more of this as she has made me miserable forever. Let me hear from you soon, Catherine, as you are my only friend. I wish your visit to Northanger is over before Captain Tilney makes his engagement public, or you will be uncomfortably circumstanced. Poor Thorpe is in town, and I dread the sight of him as his honest heart would feel so much. I have written to him and my father. Her duplicity hurts me most as she had declared herself to be attached to me till the very last, laughing at my fears. I am ashamed to think that I bore with it for so long. We parted at last by mutual consent, but I'd be happy if we had never met. I cannot expect to know another such woman! Dearest Catherine, beware how you give your heart.

DEAR CATHERINE,

God knows I have little inclination for writing. But it is my duty to tell you that everything between me and Miss Thorpe has come to an end. I left her and Bath yesterday, never to see either again. I shall not enter into particulars, as they will pain you even more. You will soon know where the blame lies; and I hope you will forgive your brother of everything but the folly of thinking that his affection was returned. Thank God I'm undeceived in time! But it is a heavy blow! That too, after father's consent was given. But no more of this as she has made me miserable forever. Let me hear from you soon, Catherine, as you are my only friend. I wish your visit to Northanger is over before Captain Tilney makes his engagement public, or you will be uncomfortably circumstanced. Poor Thorpe is in town, and I dread the sight of him as his honest heart would feel so much. I have written to him and my father. Her duplicity hurts me most as she had declared herself to be attached to me till the very last, laughing at my fears. I am ashamed to think that I bore with it for so long. We parted at last by mutual consent, but I'd be happy if we had never met. I cannot expect to know another such woman! Dearest Catherine, beware how you give your heart.

James.

'No bad news from Fullerton, I hope?' Eleanor enquired. 'I hope none of your family is ill?'

'No, they are all well. The letter was from my brother at Oxford. I do not think I shall wish for a letter again. Poor James is so unhappy. You will soon know why.'

'To have such a kind-hearted, affectionate sister must be a comfort to him under any distress,' Henry said warmly.

'I have a favour to beg. If your brother arrives here, you must give me notice of it, so I may leave.'

Eleanor and Henry were surprised, and so, Catherine gave them the letter to read, which only increased their surprise.

Eleanor and Henry comforted Catherine, but were sure that their father would never approve of Isabella. This alarmed Catherine because of the thought that she was as insignificant in terms of fortune as Isabella. There was no news of Captain Tilney for two days, and his brother and sister did not know what to think. The general, although offended at his eldest son's lack of writing, did not feel any anxiety. The general offered to visit his son

at Woodston with the ladies, and Henry was honoured and happy. Catherine was overjoyed, and a ball would not have been more welcome to her as this little trip.

They were supposed to reach Woodston on Wednesday, and Henry decided to leave on Saturday to prepare for their visit. On Wednesday, they reached Woodston after a drive of twenty miles. Henry welcomed them with his companions of solitude; a large Newfoundland puppy and three terriers.

When the general asked Catherine of her opinion of the house, she was guarded in her praise, disappointing him. But Catherine's spirits were livened on seeing a particular room. It was a pretty room with a lovely view of the meadows, although unfurnished.

'Oh! Why don't you fit up this room, Mr. Tilney? It's the prettiest room in the world!'

'I trust it will be speedily furnished,' the general said with a smile. 'It waits only for a lady's taste!'

'Well, I would never sit anywhere else if it were my house. Oh! What a sweet little cottage among those lovely apple trees. It's the prettiest cottage!'

'You like and approve it? That is enough. Henry, remember to speak to Robinson about it. The cottage remains.'

The compliment silenced Catherine, and no further opinion could be drawn out of her. A walk into the meadows and through the village, a visit to the stables, and a lovely play with a litter of new puppies, and it was four o' clock. They were to dine now, and depart at six. Never had the day passed so quickly for Catherine!

The abundance of the dinner did not surprise the general, who ate heartily. They left at six, with Catherine wondering how or when she would return to Woodston again.

Chapter Seventeen

Sent Home

The next morning, Catherine received an unexpected letter from Isabella in which she stated that she was leaving Bath. She had not heard from Catherine's brother after he had left for Oxford and she was afraid that he had misunderstood her. He was the only man she had ever loved and requested Catherine to set things right between them. Isabella maintained that she found Captain Tilney disagreeable.

Catherine concluded that Isabella was shallow and false. She was ashamed of having loved Isabella. She informed Henry and Miss Tilney about Isabella's letter, and resolved to break all ties with her. But further bad news was in store for Catherine. Eleanor approached her,

almost in tears, to declare that General Tilney had ordered Catherine to be sent home. The entire family was leaving for Hereford for a fortnight. 'Do not be so distressed, my dear Eleanor,' Catherine stated, trying to subdue her own feelings. 'I'm very sorry that we have to part so soon and so suddenly. I am not offended. I can leave on Monday.'

'Dearest Catherine, I'm afraid his orders are that you leave tomorrow morning at seven.'

Catherine was stunned. To be banished like this without an explanation, after receiving so much kindness was extreme cruelty. The worst was that no servant would accompany her on this long and tiring journey.

Catherine barely slept that night and was packed and ready at six when Eleanor arrived, eager to help and show attention. Catherine could not even say goodbye to Henry as he was away. Eleanor begged Catherine to write to her and thoughtfully provided her friend with some money for the journey. The carriage arrived at seven and as it departed, Catherine's tears could not be restrained now. She could not cry in Eleanor's presence, but now she did, as it was so humiliating to be turned out of the house in such a manner. Catherine was sure that Henry

did not know of these events. What would he think and how would he react when he knew Catherine had been treated like this by his father?

Thus, the heroine returned home and was warmly welcomed by her father, mother, Sarah, George and Harriet. By each embrace, Catherine found herself soothed and relieved completely. The joy of family life eclipsed all pains for the time being. She poured her heart after half an hour and both Mr. and Mrs. Morland agreed that General Tilney's conduct was most unworthy as a parent and a gentleman. Her parents were also sorry about James's disappointment.

'But there is no harm if the match went off, as it would not be advisable to get married to such a girl,' Mrs. Morland stated. 'After all that has happened, we cannot think well of her. James will be more discreet in life because of the foolishness of his first choice.'

Catherine could not forget Henry Tilney however, and a deep melancholy descended on her. To revive her spirits, she decided to pay the Allens a visit. Catherine was received with much kindness by the Allens, who did not take the general's behaviour too kindly as well. But Mrs.

Allen was of the opinion that Henry Tilney was a most agreeable and well-bred man.

Mrs. Morland allowed Catherine to live in silence and sadness for two days. But she gave her a gentle reproof on the third day.

'My dear Catherine, there is a time for balls and plays, and a time for work. You have had quite a long run of amusements. You must try to be useful now. I hope you are not getting tired of home, because it's not as grand as Northanger. I must give you a book to read that has a clever essay about young girls spoilt for home by great acquaintance.'

Catherine applied herself to work, but after a few minutes she again sank into languor and listlessness. Mrs. Morland immediately left the room to fetch the book she wanted to give her daughter. When she returned, she saw a visitor, a young man she had never seen before. He rose respectfully, and Catherine introduced him as 'Mr. Henry Tilney.'

The young man apologised for his arrival there, stating that he had no right to be welcomed at Fullerton after what had transpired. He gave the cause of his

intrusion as the impatience to learn if Miss Morland had reached home safely. Mrs. Morland received him warmly and thanked him for the attentions he bestowed on her daughter. She told him that friends of her children were always welcome in her house and urged him not to dwell in the past.

Henry spoke to Mrs. Morland for some time. Unfortunately, he could not meet Mr. Morland as he was away from home. He wanted to pay his respects to the Allens and asked Catherine if she would accompany him to their home. Mrs. Morland consented, thinking he had something to say to Catherine regarding his father's behaviour. But what Henry had to say was entirely different. In that short walk, he told Catherine what she already knew; that he loved her. His love was returned, and Catherine listened silently as Henry told the Allens what had happened.

When Henry had returned from Woodston, his father had informed him angrily about Miss Morland's departure and ordered him to forget her. It was actually John Thorpe who had misled the general. When the general had seen his son dancing with Miss Morland,

he had enquired who she was. Thorpe, in order to impress him, had said that she belonged to a wealthy and illustrious family. The general had at once decided to make Miss Morland his daughter-in-law. He had also invited her to Northanger for the very same reason.

But when John Thorpe's advances were rejected by Catherine, he decided to tell the general on meeting him recently that Miss Morland was actually an imposter hailing from a poor family. This enraged the general, who ordered Catherine out of the house. But Henry had refused to accompany his father to Herefordshire and decided to marry Catherine instead. Father and son had a furious argument and parted ways in a dreadful disagreement. Then Henry had started for Fullerton.

Chapter Eighteen

All's Well that Ends Well

Mr. and Mrs. Morland were greatly surprised when Henry Tilney asked for their consent to marry their eldest daughter. It had never crossed their heads that an attachment might exist on either side. But although they were pleased about the match, they said that the marriage could not take place unless the general gave his consent. The young couple, although disheartened, were not surprised at this decision. Henry returned to Woodston, while Catherine stayed back at Fullerton to cry.

Thankfully, the general's heart was softened when his daughter married a man of fortune and consequence. The viscount and viscountess then spoke on behalf of their brother-in-law and brother, Henry Tilney, to the general. They made him realise that he had been misled

by Thorpe's boast more than anything. He had done Catherine wrong by thinking she was someone else, and then behaving badly with her.

The general gave in when he learnt that Catherine's family was not really poor as Thorpe had projected them to be, and that Catherine would receive three thousand pounds when she married. He asked his son to return to Northanger soon after Eleanor's marriage. He also agreed to Henry's marriage with Catherine.

So, the bells rang, and everybody smiled; and twelve months after they had first met, Henry and Catherine were married. The dreadful delays caused by the general's cruelty did not hurt them too much in the end. To be twenty-six and eighteen years old while beginning happiness together is not bad after all! Besides, their knowledge of each other was much improved, and this added strength to their attachment as well.

I leave it to be settled then, by whomsoever it may concern, whether the objective of this work is to recommend parental tyranny or reward filial disobedience.

About the Author

▪ Jane Austen

Jane Austen was born on December 16, 1775, in Steventon, Hampshire, England. While not widely popular in her own time, Austen's comic novels of love gained popularity after 1869 and her reputation skyrocketed in the 20th century. Today, Austen is considered one of the greatest writers in English history. In 2002, the British public voted her No. 70 on a list of '100 Most Famous Britons of All Time.' Her novels are considered literary classics, bridging the gap between romance and realism.

Northanger Abbey was published by Jane's brother, Henry. It was the first of Jane Austen's novels to be completed for publication in 1803. However, it was not published until after her death in 1817. Northanger Abbey is a satire of Gothic novels which were quite popular at the time.

▪ Characters

Catherine Morland – She is the protagonist and is seventeen years old. Catherine has spent all her life in the rural area of Fullerton. Catherine's naiveté leads to her confusion and frustration. But her intelligence, wit, integrity and goodness make her win Henry's love.

Henry Tilney - He is a 26-year-old parson who is intelligent and good-natured. He is well read, but has a cynical view of human behaviour. He is often amused at the folly of others, but he takes care to gently instruct them properly, particularly in the case of the naïve Catherine.

Eleanor Tilney - She is Henry's younger sister and a shy, quiet young woman. Her reserve stops her from making many friends. Like her brothers, Eleanor is subject to the tyrannical behaviour of her father, General Tilney.

General Tilney – He is the domineering father of Henry, Eleanor and Captain Tilney. He is a widower and a materialistic man.

Isabella Thorpe – She is Mrs. Thorpe's eldest daughter, and the sister of John Thorpe. Isabella is attractive and spirited, but is also a gossip concerned with superficial things. She enjoys flirting with many young men.

John Thorpe – He is the conceited and arrogant brother of Isabella, who is as superficial as his sister. He tries to woo Catherine but fails.

James Morland – He is the brother of Catherine. James is mild-mannered and caring, like his sister. James falls for Isabella and becomes engaged to her, but breaks off the engagement when she begins a flirtation with Frederick Tilney.

■ Questions

Chapter 1

- *Describe Catherine Morland in her infancy.*
- *What happened after Catherine decided to learn music? Explain in detail.*

Chapter 2

- *Describe Catherine's experiences at the ball.*
- *What were Catherine's feelings when the ball ended?*

Chapter 3

- *Why did Henry Tilney insist that Catherine keep a journal?*
- *Where did Henry think women lacked in letter writing? Was his view justified?*

Chapter 4

- *Which old acquaintance did Mrs. Allen bump into? Why did this make her happy?*
- *Who was the new friend Catherine made? Describe the events between the two friends after they were introduced till they departed for the night.*

Chapter 5

- *Which novel was Catherine engrossed in reading? Which are the other ones that Catherine recommended to her?*
- *Which was Mrs. Morland's favourite novel? What were Isabella's views on that particular novel?*

Chapter 6

- *Why was Cheap Street so difficult to cross?*
- *Whom did Catherine and Isabella meet here? Describe in detail.*

Chapter 7

- *Why was Catherine irritated at the beginning of the dance?*
- *How did Catherine bump into Henry Tilney? Why did she decline Thorpe's offer for a dance?*

Chapter 8

- *Describe the conversation between Catherine and Miss Tilney in the Pump Room.*
- *Who interrupted Catherine while she danced with Henry? Why? How was the matter resolved?*

Chapter 9

- *Why did Catherine call on Miss Tilney the next morning? Describe what happened and her reaction after that.*
- *Why did Catherine refuse to accompany Thorpe and his party? How did Isabella try to convince her to do so? Did she succeed?*

Chapter 10

- *Who was Captain Tilney? What was Catherine's first impression of him?*
- *What message did Henry convey to Catherine on Captain Tilney's behalf? What was Catherine's reply?*

Chapter 11

- *What message did Isabella carry for Catherine from Thorpe? Describe the conversation that followed between them.*
- *Who was Isabella flirting with? Why was Catherine hurt at her behaviour?*

Chapter 12

- *What strange horror tale did Henry tell Catherine to amuse himself?*
- *What prevented Catherine from getting a good look at the abbey when she first arrived? Why did she find the abbey delightful?*

Chapter 13

- *Why was the general angry at the dinner table?*
- *Describe the experience that Catherine had on the first night at the abbey.*

Chapter 14

- *Why did the general part ways from Eleanor and Catherine? Describe in detail.*
- *Describe Catherine's feelings for the general after learning about his deceased wife.*

Chapter 15

- *What did Catherine see in Mrs. Tilney's apartment?*
- *Whom did she meet as soon as she exited the room? Describe their conversation briefly.*

Chapter 16

- *In brief, describe the contents of James's letter to Catherine.*
- *Why was Catherine so happy to visit Woodston? Describe the trip briefly.*

Chapter 17

- *What bad news did Eleanor bring Catherine? What was Catherine's reaction to this?*
- *What gentle reproof did Mrs. Morland give her daughter and why?*

Chapter 18

- *Why were Mr. and Mrs. Morland surprised when Henry wanted to marry Catherine? What was their reply?*
- *How was the general convinced to let Henry marry Catherine? Describe in detail.*